OXFORD
UNIVERSITY PRESS

Great Clarendon Street, Oxford OX2 6DP

Oxford University Press is a department of the University of Oxford.
It furthers the University's objective of excellence in research, scholarship,
and education by publishing worldwide in

Oxford New York

Athens Auckland Bangkok Bogotá Buenos Aires
Cape Town Chennai Dar es Salaam Delhi Florence Hong Kong Istanbul
Karachi Kolkata Kuala Lumpur Madrid Melbourne Mexico City Mumbai
Nairobi Paris São Paulo Shanghai Singapore Taipei Tokyo Toronto Warsaw

with associated companies in Berlin Ibadan

Oxford is a registered trade mark of Oxford University Press
in the UK and in certain other countries

British Library Cataloguing in Publication Data available

ISBN 0 19 272504 1

1 3 5 7 9 10 8 6 4 2

Printed in Malaysia

FRANKENSTEIN

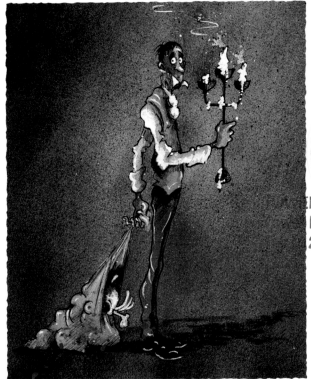

Adapted and Illustrated by
Chris Mould

OXFORD
UNIVERSITY PRESS

Time stood still while we were trapped on the ice. We heard and saw nothing. My mind took me on many a journey but still I returned to this limbo, locked in until the thaw came.

One evening we saw a figure drifting towards us on the ice. We pulled him onto the deck and he whispered his name . . . 'Victor . . . Victor Frankenstein.'

We took him to my cabin, where he told me his strange and harrowing story.

Victor Frankenstein's Story

I was born in Geneva and my memories are happy ones. When I was five my mother adopted the foster child of a poor family with many children. The girl's name was Elizabeth and we loved her as if she were one of us.

Later, my mother had two more sons, Ernest and William. A young woman called Justine came to help us, and she too became one of the family.

At school my greatest friend was Henry Clerval. I studied hard at school, and from an early age the secrets of life itself became my passion, and I read many books on the subject.

When I was fifteen I observed a most violent storm, seeing a huge tree reduced to nothing by a bolt of lightning. Now I knew its power, I decided I must study electricity.

For seventeen years I was happy. But then, my mother became ill. It was her dying wish that one day Elizabeth and I would marry.

Not long after my mother's death, I had to leave for Ingoldstadt where I was to attend the university. My new surroundings soon helped to dim the sad memory of the world I had left behind me.

I attended my lectures in science and chemistry with great enthusiasm. The structure of the human frame, and especially life itself, became the focus of my study. I searched for the answer to life and death. I did not know that one day my efforts would destroy me and everything I had.

For two years I did not rest. Above my laboratory towered a tall electric mast to catch lightning to use in my machines.

My mind was filled with my obsession. I could think of nothing else—except the creation of a human being. And so I began my work.

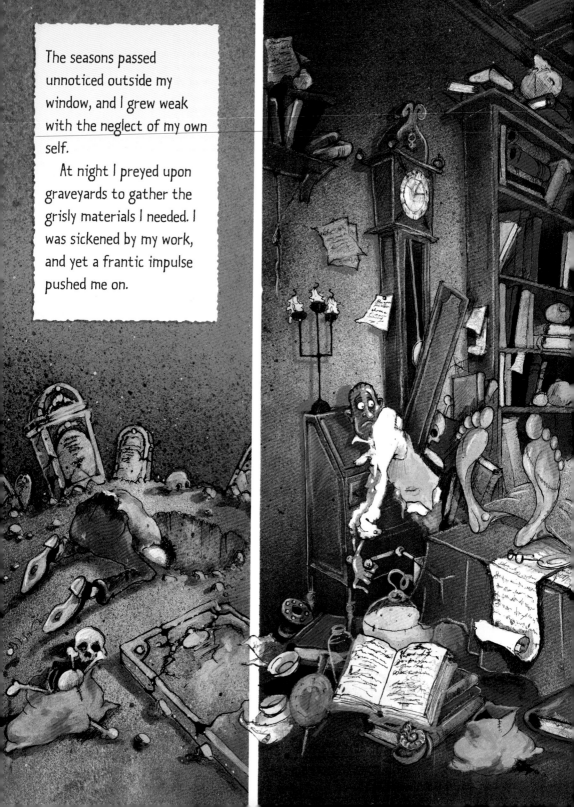

The seasons passed unnoticed outside my window, and I grew weak with the neglect of my own self.

At night I preyed upon graveyards to gather the grisly materials I needed. I was sickened by my work, and yet a frantic impulse pushed me on.

It was on a stormy November night that my work drew to a close. I worked until the early hours of the morning as I tried to spark life in my creation. To my astonishment, I saw the eye of the creature open. It lived!

Suddenly I came to my senses. I had created a monster! Unable to look at the creature, I locked the room and left. I lay on my bed, exhausted, but I slept badly. When I awoke, there was the creature looming over me.

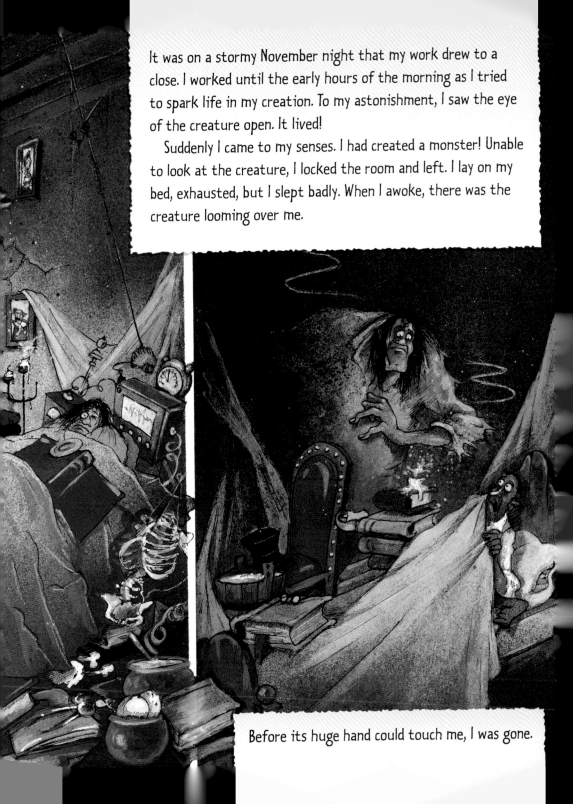

Before its huge hand could touch me, I was gone.

I wandered the town, and in my daze, I did not notice a train arrive from Geneva. Suddenly my good friend Henry Clerval ran towards me.

'I have good news,' he said. 'Your family are well, and I am to join you at the university.'

We returned happily to my house, where I asked him to wait outside in case the monster was waiting.

But he had gone. I pushed away all thoughts of the creature and soon we were laughing and joking. Then, suddenly, I fell to the floor in a fit. For two months, Henry nursed me day and night.

Then, one day, my father wrote to say that my brother William had been murdered.

We left for Geneva, and, as we rode into town, I saw the creature. Was he the murderer? I could not doubt it.

It was an unhappy reunion for my family.

'We were out walking,' said my father. 'The children were playing hide and seek. William disappeared. I found him at five o'clock in the morning. We think someone killed him to steal the gold chain he wore around his neck.'

The chain was found in Justine's pocket. She was arrested.

We all knew Justine was not capable of murder. Only I knew the truth, but who would believe me?

Justine was found guilty and was sent away to a dark cell where she waited quietly for her death. She would die because of me, just as William had died because of me.

I became ill again and even Elizabeth's love could not help me.
I walked alone for days and days among the Alps. One morning
I saw a figure heading towards me. Moving fast, it jumped over
the rocks. It was the monster I had created!

'You are evil!' I cried. 'You have killed those I love!'

'You are less unhappy than I,' he replied. 'William and Justine
died because you did not show me love. There is something you
must do for me.'

We sat by a fire and he began.

The Creature's Story

When I left your home I walked for many days until I found a village. But the people chased and threw stones at me. I escaped, and moved on to an empty hut, built up against a cottage. From a distance, I watched the old man, the boy, and the girl who lived there.

I learnt much by watching and listening to them. I learnt how to talk. I saw their faces were beautiful, but when I saw my reflection in a pool it was terrible. They must never see me. I saw love and friendship, and felt lonelier and lonelier.

I understood that the old man was blind. It would be safe to approach him whilst he was alone. I knocked at his door in the guise of a traveller in need of rest. But when the others returned they recoiled in horror and the boy beat me with his stick. I escaped and left.

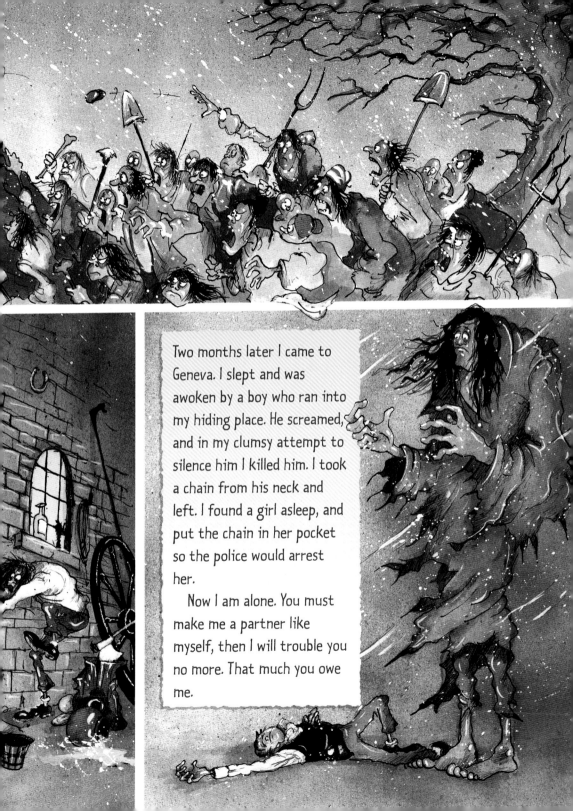

Two months later I came to Geneva. I slept and was awoken by a boy who ran into my hiding place. He screamed, and in my clumsy attempt to silence him I killed him. I took a chain from his neck and left. I found a girl asleep, and put the chain in her pocket so the police would arrest her.

Now I am alone. You must make me a partner like myself, then I will trouble you no more. That much you owe me.

Frankenstein Continues His Story

I thought long and hard and though I hated the idea I gave my word.

'But promise that then you will disappear,' I said.

He agreed and left.

I decided to go to England to continue my work, promising to marry Elizabeth on my return. Henry travelled with me and together we went to England and then onto Scotland.

The following morning held a dreadful shock. The police arrested me for a murder the previous night, as my actions had been suspicious. They took me to see the body, and to my horror it was my dear friend Henry Clerval. I was thrown into a cell. The monster had struck again.

As I worked I began to feel remorse. One night, I looked out of the window, and there he stood, watching me. I threw down my tools, abandoning my new creation.

The creature roared with anger. 'I will be with you on your wedding night!' he shouted, disappearing into the fog. I took a boat and dropped all traces of my work into the loch.

The magistrate realized that I could not have committed the crime. I grieved for my friend Henry, but the arrival of my father lifted my spirits. He gave me the good news that Elizabeth and Ernest were safe and well. We set sail for Geneva.

When we arrived in Geneva, Elizabeth was there to meet me. We arranged our wedding, but I feared for our lives as I remembered the words of the monster.

After the wedding we left for a honeymoon at a peaceful hotel. Finally I could feel happy.

Elizabeth went to bed, but I went outside with my gun. Then I heard a scream.

Elizabeth lay cold and dead on the bed.

When I awoke the next morning I felt the full horror of what had happened. My life would never be the same.

Suddenly I had an awful thought. What if the monster was even now murdering my father and my brother Ernest as I lay here on my bed?

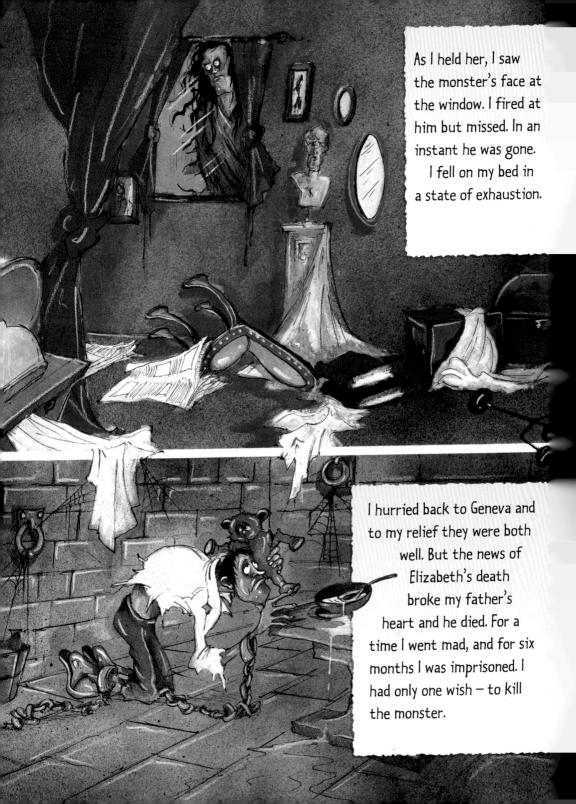

As I held her, I saw the monster's face at the window. I fired at him but missed. In an instant he was gone.

I fell on my bed in a state of exhaustion.

I hurried back to Geneva and to my relief they were both well. But the news of Elizabeth's death broke my father's heart and he died. For a time I went mad, and for six months I was imprisoned. I had only one wish — to kill the monster.

I decided to leave Geneva for ever and pursue the monster. He went north, to the ice and snow, for I would feel the cold, while he would not.

Only when I slept was I happy. I dreamed of Elizabeth, Henry, and my family. Soon I would join them in death.

I was losing hope when I saw a familiar shape in the distance. As I got closer the ice broke and he was carried away by the sea.

I drifted along on another piece of ice. I was sure I would drown. It was then I saw your ship.

I know I have not long to live, but I do not fear death. I ask you to kill this monster. There is no more I can say.

Poor Victor. He worked so hard to achieve something that, in the end, he lost everything. He died a few minutes after finishing his story.

Later, I heard a voice from the cabin where his body lay. Inside was a large creature, holding him close. 'So I have killed you, too. Forgive me,' he wept. 'Understand one thing,' he said, turning to me. 'I have suffered more than anyone. My heart, like yours, was made for love, but no one would let me love. I hate myself more than anyone hates me, and now my own death is near.'

'I shall go north across the ice and build a great fire. There I will lie down and die.'

The monster sprang from the window and clambered onto the ice as he said his last words.

The sea carried him away and he was lost in the darkness.